Puffin Books

Cockawun and Cockatoo

Sulphur-crested Cockawun and Cockatoo are rescued as nestlings from the site of the first Parliament House in Canberra. Arthur rears the young birds and they all grow up together in a new farm in the mountains.

Cockatoo has a wild streak and flies off to join a flock in the bush. Cockawun, however, prefers human company. But with his mischievious ways he wreaks havoc around the house and farm. Arthur has to fight for his pet to stay in the family.

Cockawun soon proves himself, and the two become lifelong companions. Eventually Arthur takes Cockawun back to Canberra for a memorable visit to his birthplace.

Based on a true story, *Cockawun and Cockatoo* is a moving and evocative new novel from Christobel Mattingley.

Also by Christobel Mattingley

No Gun for Asmir
Asmir in Vienna
Escape from Sarajevo
The Sack
Work Wanted

For younger readers

Ginger
Hurry Up, Alice!

CHRISTOBEL MATTINGLEY

Cockawun and Cockatoo

WITH ILLUSTRATIONS BY SUSY BOYER RIGBY

Puffin Books

To George Coleman who began the story and to Erica Irving who encouraged me to finish it.

Puffin Books
Penguin Books Australia Ltd
487 Maroondah Highway, PO Box 257
Ringwood, Victoria 3134, Australia
Penguin Books Ltd
Harmondsworth, Middlesex, England
Penguin Putnam Inc.
375 Hudson Street, New York, New York 10014, USA
Penguin Books Canada Limited
10 Alcorn Avenue, Toronto, Ontario, Canada, M4V 3B2
Penguin Books (N.Z.) Ltd
Cnr Rosedale and Airborne Roads, Albany, Auckland, New Zealand
Penguin Books (South Africa) (Pty) Ltd
5 Watkins Street, Denver, Ext 4 2094, South Africa
Penguin Books India (P) Ltd
11, Community Centre, Panchsheel Park, New Delhi 110 017, India

First published by Penguin Books, 1999
10 9 8 7 6 5 4 3 2 1

Designed by Cathy Larsen, Penguin Design Studio
Typeset in 14/18pt Bembo by Midland Typesetters, Maryborough, Victoria
Made and printed in Australia by Australian Print Group, Maryborough, Victoria

National Library of Australia
Cataloguing-in-Publication data:

Mattingley, Christobel, 1931–.
Cockawun and Cockatoo.

ISBN 0 14 130157 0.

I. Rigby, Susy Boyer. II. Title.
A823.3

www.puffin.com.au

Contents

A New Home

Once upon a time, where Canberra's first Parliament House now stands, there grew a tree. A great gum tree.

It had been growing there for hundreds of years before white people came to Australia. It had given shade and firewood to countless generations of the first Australians, food and shelter for flocks of parrots, families of possums, and a host of lizards, beetles and spiders. Kookaburras laughed among its broad branches and cockatoos nested in its hollow limbs. It was a grand old tree.

But one day white men decided that the place where it grew was the very place for the

Parliament House, the centre of the new city of Canberra, from which all Australia would be governed.

So they cut the tree down.

When the tree lay fallen, one of the men discovered, in a broken spout, two baby cockatoos, huddled together like floppy pink pincushions, with their first feathers pricking through their scrawny skins.

'Poor little fellas,' he said, and put them in his pocket. 'But I know someone who will be your friend.' He took them home to Sydney and gave them to his nephew, Arthur Wiseman.

Arthur raided the chooks' food and made a porridge of pollard and crushed wheat for Cockawun and Cockatoo, feeding them a dozen times a day until they were able to feed themselves.

They grew fast and soon began to forage for themselves. Arthur proudly watched over his pets, sleek and snowy in their new-fledged plumage. He had always envied the boy next-door his fantail pigeons. But the cockatoos were far more beautiful, with their curling crests of sharp lemon-yellow and the softness of lemon squash under their wide white wings.

Arthur loved to watch the pigeons wheeling in the sky or clustering like snowballs along the roof ridge. But he wondered as he watched his cockatoos in the plum tree, if they would always be contented with backyards and rooftops like the pigeons. And he wished for space and big gum trees.

While the cockatoos were still quite young, Arthur's wish came true. His father, who had grown up in the country, grew tired of the noise of the city with all its cars and people. He found a farm carved out of the rainforest high up in the mountains and he took his family there.

It was a long journey by train. The children, their luggage, and Cockawun and Cockatoo in a thick cardboard carton, crammed into the compartment. Arthur's mother handed round cheese and pickle sandwiches, but Arthur was too excited to eat as they rumbled north through suburbs and more suburbs of houses twinkling among the trees, onwards through dark bush where only stars twinkled, across a big bridge over a wide slow river shining in the moonlight.

One by one, the children, their mother, their father, and even Arthur at last dropped asleep as the train swayed northwards through the night, still northwards. But underneath Arthur's seat Cockawun and Cockatoo were busy in their box, shredding the stout cardboard with their even stronger beaks, chewing their way to freedom.

When Arthur awoke, Cockawun and Cockatoo were sitting on the luggage rack opposite, looking down at him with their bright black eyes. Arthur laughed, and they began to dance, spreading their tails, nodding their heads, raising their crests, squawking joyously.

'Hush! Cocky, hush!' Arthur said as he saw the conductor in the corridor.

The conductor had heard the noise and was coming to investigate. 'Pets not allowed to travel with passengers,' he said sternly. 'They should be in the guard's van.'

But when Cockawun sidled up to him and pleaded, 'Pretty Cocky, scratch Cocky,' he smiled. He looked at the family's tickets and said, 'Well ... as it's not much further ... we won't worry this time.' He scratched Cockawun in his favourite place behind his crest and said to Mr Wiseman, 'They're healthy young 'uns.

They'll see you out. I've got an old fella at home, belonged to my uncle. Must be seventy, if it's a day. Well, good luck, wherever you're going.'

'To the Bulga,' said Mr Wiseman.

'Up above Dingo Creek? Rugged country. You'll be glad of your son.'

Arthur squared his shoulders.

Just after the sun had risen over misty river flats where cows were grazing, the family got off the train and packed themselves and their belongings into the car which was to take them to their new home.

Soon the gentle grassy slopes were behind them and the road climbed up, curling like a stockwhip across the back of the ranges. Cockawun and Cockatoo, now in a wooden crate lashed to the running board, put their eyes to the cracks and peered out at the bush they had never known – the towering tallow woods and the big brush box trees bold against the sky, the dark-stemmed ironbarks and white-trunked snappy gums.

Higher and higher they climbed, past banks bowered with ferns, and gullies secret with moss and trickling streams, until the valley below and the mountains beyond were blue with the mystery of distance. The air was sharp with the scent of eucalyptus, ringing with the notes of a myriad birds. Cockawun and Cockatoo quivered with the excitement of all the new smells and sounds.

And when a flock of white cockatoos flew across the treetops, their harsh wild cries echoing down the valley, Cockatoo stretched her wings and called back to her own kind with all her heart. But Cockawun, who had already learned human talk, raised his crest and screeched, 'Ta-ta. Cocky want a biscuit.'

The rough road ended, but still they jolted on along a track the timber-cutters had made with their bullock teams. The farm was an uplands outpost, its buildings clustered like a stockade in the clearing. The house, barn, cow bails, stable and stockyard had all been built from the giant trees felled to make way for the rough paddocks.

Right to the post and rail fences the surviving forest stood its ground, ready still to ambush unwary intruders with thorny thickets and sting-ing trees, noose-like vines and hidden gullies. It had been a battlefield for the first white settlers. But twenty years of steel and fire had made their mark on centuries of growing, and now cows grazed where mighty blackbutts had stood, potatoes grew where red cedars had reached for the sky, and scarecrows stuck out their stiff arms where manferns had waved their graceful fronds.

Arthur gazed around in awe. It was all so different from anything he had ever seen. His father began unloading the car. His mother carried the hamper into the house and his sister Dorothy followed with an armful of bundles, while baby Ellie sat in the grass watching a bright blue jewel beetle.

But Arthur's first concern was to show Cockawun and Cockatoo their new home. He undid the rope lashings and prised up the boards across the top of the crate. Cockawun and Cockatoo clambered out, stretched their wings, then took flight. Arthur watched in silent delight as, calling joyously, they circled the clearing, gleaming white against the dark green forest. Then, although the sun was warm and soft as wool on his skin, Arthur felt a cold tremor of fear at the sudden thought that they might not return.

But they did. As the family settled into the house, Cockawun and Cockatoo found a place for themselves on the verandah railing. Cockatoo often moved out into the pear tree when flocks of king parrots flew in to feast. But Cockawun preferred to perch on the back of a chair by the kitchen window, where he could see and hear the family as they sat around the table.

Cockatoo always answered when a flock of white cockatoos came over, calling raucously, and sometimes she flew off after them into the forest.

But Cockawun took no notice of his wild cousins. He was more interested in his human family and all they did and said. He followed Arthur every morning and evening to the cow bails and sat on the top rail of the yard watching

Rusty the dog moving the cows in and out. When Snowy the cat came in for her share of the sweet warm milk, he would say, 'Cocky want a drink.'

He investigated and declared a truce with the big diamond-patterned carpet snake and left it to lie quietly looped over the cowshed rafters in the daytime and to go about its business at night, sliding silently down to hunt rats in the haybales. But he made friends with Black Jack, the horse in the stable, and always followed the plough to pick up anything he fancied from the new-turned earth.

He hissed when the sleepy lizards emerged from under the verandah, but did not interfere with them, even when they made inroads on the strawberries or gorged on the windfall cherry plums, which he also enjoyed. Snakes in the grass, however, were a different matter. Then he really set off the alarm, shrieking 'Snake! Snake!' until someone came.

One day when Cockatoo heard the call of her own kind she flew away and didn't come back. The next day there was a great storm, the greatest Arthur had ever known. Storm clouds piled up on the mountains, thunder rolled over the valleys shaking the house on its wooden stumps. And lightning struck three trees, three giant tallow woods growing along the old Aboriginal trail across the ridge.

Arthur worried about Cockatoo and wondered if he would ever see her again.

Mischief!

Cockawun missed Cockatoo also. He moped and grew miserable, even though Arthur petted him and the family made a fuss of him. Then he became mischievous.

Sometimes he would steal Rusty's bones. Or he would creep up on Rusty while he was asleep and make possum noises. Rusty would wake up in a frenzy of barking and rush off wildly, scattering the chooks in a squawking flurry. One day Rusty rushed straight through Mrs Wiseman's legs as she was carrying skim milk to the pigs. 'Bad dog,' Mrs Wiseman scolded, jumping with surprise. The buckets slipped, slopping milk over her skirt and into her boots. 'Now look what you've done,' she said crossly. Rusty barked at Cockawun. Mrs Wiseman looked around. 'So it's you again, Cocky. I might have known it. It's not poor Rusty's fault at all.' Then she laughed. 'It's no good crying over spilt milk. But you're a bad boy, Cocky.'

Cockawun also learned to tease Snowy. When she was sleeping peacefully in the sun, he would sneak up and nip her tail. She would race off squalling in rage, and one day she scratched baby Ellie, who tried to catch her.

Cockawun would sit quietly on the verandah railing, looking as if butter wouldn't melt in his beak, watching all the commotion he had caused.

One morning after he had pulled the pegs off Mrs Wiseman's washing so that all the sheets fell in the dirt, she was really upset. 'That Cocky will have to go,' she said.

'No, Mum, no,' Arthur pleaded. 'I'll help you wash the sheets again. And I'll help you hang them out.'

'We-e-ell,' said his mother. 'I'll be glad of that and it's fine for today. But you know how often I have to wash.'

'I could take him for a walk on wash days,' Arthur said.

'You've got your schoolwork to do,' his mother reminded him. 'You'll have to think of something else to keep that bird out of mischief.'

Arthur carried buckets of rainwater from the tank to the copper, cut firewood and stoked the fire underneath the copper. Then he helped his mother shake the sheets and brush the worst of the mud off them before they pushed them into the copper.

'I'll stir and I'll stoke,' Arthur volunteered. So he stood and stirred the sheets in the steaming water with the long smooth pole cut from the bush and stripped of its bark. And from time to time he bent down and put on more sticks of dry wood to keep the fire dancing bright under the old copper.

His mother wouldn't let him lift the sheets out of the scalding water. But he filled the tub with more buckets full of rainwater for rinsing. Then he turned the handle of the mangle while his mother fed the sheets through the rollers for the second time. He gripped one end of the laden clothes basket while his mother took the other, and together they carried it to the line stretched between the trees.

While his mother started hanging out the sheets again, Arthur fetched Cockawun. He showed Cockawun a peg. Cockawun reached out for it and Arthur said, 'No. Naughty Cocky.' He took Cockawun up to the clothes line.

'Arthur,' his mother shouted. 'Keep that bird away from my washing.'

'It's all right, Mum,' Arthur said. 'He's not stupid. I'm just teaching him.' And when Cockawun reached again for a peg holding a newly washed pillowcase, Arthur said, 'No' sharply and pulled him away.

Up and down the clothes line they went until Cockawun lost interest in the enticing little round knobs all along it. From the tone of Arthur's voice Cockawun knew it was not a game Arthur was playing. So he ended the lesson of his own accord and flew up into the pear tree.

But soon he found new ways to amuse himself. He discovered the walnuts ripening on the old tree beyond the barn and revelled in cracking them open, quietly gorging unnoticed until Mr Wiseman happened to come across him. 'You wretched bird,' he shouted in exasperation. 'Those walnuts were going to buy boots for the children!'

So Arthur took to feeding Cockawun bones from his mother's stockpot, and Cockawun would stay out of mischief for hours, biting on the bones busily with his big black beak. Arthur also fixed a perch beside the mirror on the verandah where his father shaved in the morning, and Cockawun loved to sit and peer at his reflection and talk to himself. He also loved to listen to the gramophone, cocking his head to try to discover the source of the sound, and he and Ellie would dance for as long as Arthur or Dorothy would turn the handle.

Sometimes Cockawun took himself off to the edge of the bush. He stole the blue berries and shards of blue china from among the snail shells and chook feathers decorating the playground of the satin bowerbird. And Arthur's little sister Dorothy cried at their loss. She loved to watch the handsome glossy blue-black bowerbird arranging and re-arranging his treasures and performing his display.

When she sobbed out the story to her mother,

Mrs Wiseman was annoyed. 'That Cocky's into everything! I've just about had enough of him!'

Then Cockawun started on the pumpkins that Arthur's father had put to dry on the shed roof. First he gnawed off the stems with his strong sharp beak. Then he cut into the tough blue rind until he reached the bright orange flesh.

Arthur discovered what Cockawun had been up to when his mother sent him out to fetch a pumpkin for dinner. He didn't know what to do. He knew how precious each pumpkin was. His father had counted them all and was proud he'd grown enough to last the family all winter. No use hiding it or throwing it away. Besides, that would be a waste. If his mother cut away the part that Cockawun had chewed, they could eat the rest.

He decided to take the damaged pumpkin into the kitchen. 'Look, Mum, the possums have been at the pumpkin.'

Just at that moment his father came in. 'Possums? Possums at the pumpkins? Let's have a look.' He grabbed the pumpkin from Arthur. 'Possums!' he exploded. 'It's that Cockawun! I'll possum him when I get my hands on him!'

'No, Dad, no!' Arthur screamed, as his father strode out onto the verandah.

Cockawun took flight with a shriek.

Arthur caught up to his father, who was shaking his fist towards the pear tree. 'Dad, he doesn't mean to be naughty. He hasn't unpegged the clothes once since I taught him it was naughty. I'll teach him about the pumpkins.'

Arthur's father growled. 'All right,' he said grudgingly. 'But I'm warning you, it's the last time. Any more trouble and I'll wring his neck.'

'Yes, Dad, I know. I promise I'll keep him out of trouble.'

'Trouble is, you don't know what you're trying to promise,' his father grumbled.

The family sat silently round the table over the meal. Arthur's dad had just killed a sheep, and roast mutton and baked potatoes and pumpkin were a treat. But Arthur had difficulty swallowing. Even his mum's special custard and stewed pears didn't slip down as quickly and easily as they usually did. And he passed on the cream. Watching it spread white over the yellow custard made him think of Cockawun. Cocka-wun with his neck wrung.

He jumped up from the table. ''Scuse me, Mum.' He had to go and see that Cockawun was all right, that he was not up to any other mischief.

At first he couldn't find him. He wasn't on the verandah rail. He wasn't in the pear tree. He wasn't on the cow-yard fence. And thank goodness, he wasn't on the clothes line. Or the shed roof among the pumpkins. But where was he? Oh, where was he?

'Cockawun, Cockawun, where are you?' Arthur called.

He heard a familiar sound, 'Ta-ta!' from the verandah and looked up. Cockawun was on the roof, nibbling away at a rusty patch over the kitchen door.

'Cockawun! Cockawun! Stop that! Oh, stop it!'

Arthur's father came out onto the verandah. 'What's he up to now?' He looked up and saw Cockawun's eye peering down through the hole in the rusty iron. 'Ta-ta!' Cockawun said cheerily.

'It'll be ta-ta for you when I get my hands on you,' Arthur's father roared. 'As if this place isn't hard enough work without all the trouble you cause. Why didn't you fly off with the wild birds like Cockatoo? Why did you choose to hang about here and make a pest of yourself? Fetch him down, Arthur. That roof won't take my weight.'

Reluctantly Arthur climbed onto the veran-dah rail and shinned up the post to the corner of the roof. 'Come on, Cocky,' he coaxed. 'Cocky want a biscuit?'

Cockawun sidled over trustingly. Arthur picked him up, feeling like a murderer as he handed him over. 'Here he is, Dad. But please, Dad. Don't hurt him. I'll teach him about the roof *and* the pumpkins. He really is clever. He won't touch them once he knows.' Hollow with unhappiness, he stared pleadingly at his father.

All the family were on the verandah now. Dorothy was twisting her hair, looking on with big eyes. Even Ellie was quiet, sucking her thumb furiously. Rusty and Snowy watched from a safe distance. Arthur's mother looked at her husband. 'Give the boy a chance. He loves that bird.'

Everyone held their breath. Even the cat stopped twitching her tail.

Arthur's dad glared at Cockawun, then unclenched his fists. 'All right,' he muttered. 'You've got one more chance, bird.' He didn't look at Arthur, but turned and went inside.

Arthur put Cockawun on the verandah rail and ran after his father. 'I'll fix the roof, Dad, and I'll make sure Cockawun behaves. And I'll make you and Mum a cup of tea now.' He bustled about topping up the big black kettle and bringing in more wood for the stove. Dorothy set out the cups and fetched the milk. Even Ellie helped, teetering to her father with the sugar bowl.

Their dad sat with his elbows on the table. 'I've been thinking I'd try a patch of early potatoes. If I keep them well covered I might be able to beat the frost.'

'I'll help you, Dad,' Arthur said quickly.

So Arthur and his dad worked together preparing the soil, setting the potato pieces in raised rows and cutting bracken in the bush to cover them and protect them from the frost. Armful after armful of crisp brown bracken fronds Arthur carried and laid over the mounds.

'We might even try some peas,' his dad said. 'New potatoes and peas'd go well with spring lamb, don't you think?'

Arthur nodded. If only Cockawun didn't get to them first. If only . . .

Last Chance!

Before Arthur had a chance to rub Cockawun's beak in a pumpkin and scold him, his dad decided it was time to put the pumpkins in the shed. 'If Cocky can get the stalks off them, they're dry enough to store.'

'I'll do it, Dad,' Arthur volunteered. He climbed onto the roof and passed the precious pumpkins down one by one to his father, who loaded them into the barrow. Then Arthur jumped down and trundled them to the shed, with Cocky sitting on the wheelguard in front, swaying with excitement.

'They're not for you, Cocky,' Arthur told him

as he arranged the big bulging grey shapes carefully on the shelf. Three trips it took before the summer harvest was safely stored for winter. Arthur closed the shed door and propped the wheelbarrow against it. Cockawun couldn't move *that*! But the latch was another matter. It might be just the new challenge Cockawun was after.

Arthur fished about in his pockets. String was no good. Cocky would bite through that in a minute. Wire was what it needed. Arthur looked around and pulled down a piece stuck between two log slabs. He pushed it through the hasp and twisted it round the latch. 'You'll only blunt your beak on that, my friend,' he said to Cockawun, who was riding on his shoulder. 'So don't touch,' he said sternly, as if he was teaching Ellie.

Next there was the hole in the verandah roof to repair. Arthur found the top off a kerosene tin his father had used to make a bucket. That should cover the hole. But how to make it stay in place? Arthur decided a stone would do the job. Cockawun came with him while he hunted for one the right size, then flew on to the roof while Arthur was still wondering how to get it up. The boy scowled at the bird. 'It's all your fault. And how am I going to do it? No use throwing it. It'd only make another hole.'

Just then his dad came by. 'Need a hand, son?'

'Yes, please, Dad.'

His father passed up the stone and Arthur put the tin patch over the hole. 'That should do it,' he said. 'Just don't you take a fancy to the roof again,' he told Cockawun sternly.

Tea that night was a cheerful meal. The thunder that had been muttering and grumbling in the mountains beyond the plateau suddenly came closer, herding the rain clouds ahead of it. Soon they seemed to pause right above the house and let down their burden, as if to escape.

Arthur raced out to the verandah. Not a drop was leaking through his patch. Water was gurgling into the tanks by the house and his mother was smiling. No need to carry water from the creek for a while. Plenty now for the washing. His dad came out and surveyed the deluge. Water was cascading off the shed roof, running down the furrows of the newly dug potato patch.

'Just got the pumpkins moved in the nick of

time,' he said. 'And the potatoes planted.' He grinned at Cockawun, who was sitting in the rain squawking with the pleasure of it and flapping his wings. 'Thanks to you, you barmy bird.'

Arthur felt Cockawun had won a reprieve and he slept easy that night. And for days afterwards the threat to Cocky's neck seemed to have lifted.

The bush was fragrant with new scents, new life after the rain, and Cockawun went off for one of his rare times in the wild. He followed a flock of yellow-tailed black cockatoos and foraged with them as they stripped bark off forest trees searching for grubs. Then he met up with some red-tailed black cockatoos and feasted with them on the glossy berries that festooned the creepers.

But he didn't find any of his own kind and after a few days he drifted back to his family.

Arthur was delighted to see him. 'I knew you'd be back,' he whispered as he scratched behind Cockawun's shining golden crest. 'I knew. Dad said, "Good riddance" and Mum said, "At last it's safe to hang out my best lace cloth on the line and know it won't all be unravelled by that pesky bird when I come to fetch it in." But I knew you'd be back. I knew.'

Cockawun put his head on one side and gave the little secret whistling breath of contentment, which only Arthur knew. 'Cocky's a good boy,' Arthur said, and Cockawun danced in agreement, raising his crest, spreading his wings.

'Cocky, you're a clown,' Arthur's dad laughed.

Arthur's mum said, 'You're more mischief than three children and a dog and a cat all rolled into one, but I missed you.' She gave him a piece of bread and his favourite strawberry jam.

The next morning Arthur was getting on with his schoolwork at the kitchen table. It was going well now that he wasn't worrying all the time about Cockawun being out in the bush. Dorothy was sitting beside him with her copybook. Even Ellie had her little slate and was pretending to write.

Then suddenly there was the stamping of angry boots on the wooden verandah floor, the shouting of an angry farmer, a father with five people to feed.

'That darn bird! That's the end of him! I've been patient too long. Too long. Just as the potatoes were beginning to shoot. I'll shoot *him*, see if I don't.'

Arthur threw down his pencil. His exercise book fell to the floor as he jumped up. He raced to the high shelf where his father kept his gun and dragged a chair in front of it. Standing on the chair, he challenged his father.

'No, Dad, no! You can't shoot Cockawun. You can't.'

Dorothy ran to stand beside the chair. Ellie began to cry. His mother picked her up and stepped forward. Rusty the dog began to howl, and Snowy the cat, who spent all her waking moments trying to avoid or outwit the bird, began to yowl in sympathy. For a moment Arthur felt dizzy, dizzy with fear, with horror. His dad was a good shot. He was deadly on the currawongs that raided the fruit trees. And on the crows that came after the lambs. Deadly.

But Cockawun was no cowardly killer picking on helpless creatures. Cockawun was clever and observant and determined. He was mischievous but not malicious. 'Dad,' Arthur pleaded. 'Don't shoot Cockawun. Please, Dad.' He felt his voice choking and couldn't go on.

He couldn't put into words the thought of life without Cockawun.

His dad dropped down in the chair by the table and slumped on to Arthur's arithmetic book. 'You're all against me, aren't you?' he said, looking round at the accusing faces. 'But I'm only trying to make a living for us all. And now the potatoes are ruined.'

'I'll plant them again, Dad. I'll do it now.'

'There's nothing left to plant. That devil of a bird has chewed them all up. I caught him at it red-handed.'

Arthur began to splutter. He couldn't help it. The thought of Cockawun red-handed . . .

'It's no laughing matter, Arthur,' his mother said, but Arthur knew she was having trouble not laughing.

Suddenly his dad saw the joke and began to laugh, too. 'A red-handed cockatoo! Now there's a thought! We could sell him to a circus. Or a sideshow. For a fortune. He could be a star turn.'

Although his father was laughing, Arthur was horribly afraid. Shooting Cockawun? Wringing his neck? Selling him? He couldn't bear the thought of any of them.

'I was only joking,' his father said. 'But I'm serious about getting rid of him.'

'You won't shoot him?' Arthur whispered, dizzy again with fear.

'No, so you can come down off the chair.'

'And you won't wring his neck?'

His dad shook his head. Arthur climbed down.

'But I tell you what I will do. I'm going to town tomorrow and I'll find someone there who'll take him.'

Arthur stared at his father in disbelief. Cockawun in a town? With cars and people and noise and houses everywhere? Cockawun in a cage? With a locked door and poo on the floor? Cockawun on a chain? With his wings clipped? No one could do that to Cockawun. No one.

He fled from the kitchen without a word, took a piece of cheese and some cold potatoes from the safe on the verandah, and ran to the pear tree. Cockawun was sitting on his favourite bough.

'Cocky want a ride?' Arthur asked, and Cockawun hopped on to his shoulder.

Arthur thought he heard his mother calling,

heard his sisters crying, heard his father shouting. But the blood was drumming in his ears, his heart was thumping as he ran, ran, ran, with Cockawun clinging to his shirt. Ran on and on into the secret sacred embrace of the ancient bush still unvanquished by axe, saw or fire.

Escape to the Forest

At last Arthur paused and looked around. Cockawun nibbled his ear and tweaked his sweaty hair. 'Cocky's a good boy,' he said as he took off from Arthur's shoulder. The big white bird circled the boy twice before heading off through the tall tallow woods, flying slowly enough for Arthur to keep up.

On they went and on, until Arthur lost all sense of time, all sense of direction. He felt as if he were in a dream among the towering age-old trees. Suddenly, although it was growing late, it also became lighter as Cockawun flew into a clearing.

A great tree stood in the centre, encircled by stones. Arthur felt as if he had known the place for ever. And ever. And ever. As if its wisdom was running in his blood along the secret pathways through his mind and spirit. As if its stillness was enfolding him in its warmth, like a possum-skin cloak wrapped grey and cloud-soft around him. He walked slowly to the great tree and looked up at it in awe. Cockawun had settled on an outer branch, high up like a sentinel.

Arthur sank down at its foot, suddenly tired with a grief too big to bear. An old grief. A deep deep loss that had no words. He slipped into an exhausted sleep confused with dreams, while Cockawun watched over him from the tree top, and thunderclouds gathered on a distant range.

The wind was singing an ancient song louder and louder through the twisting branches. A song that pulsed through Arthur's dreams of men adorned with white ochre and white and yellow feathers, and boys becoming men while flames flickered and flared.

And as Arthur slept, sharp shining knives of lightning cleaved orange slices through the grey

pumpkin thunderclouds, and the rain began to fall in seed-shaped drops, heavy, heavier, laden with the weight of oceans, washing like a tide over shores of leaves.

Arthur lay huddled at the foot of the great tree. He did not stir as the storm battled the forest and as the rain soaked through his shirt, through his singlet, through his trousers, into his boots. Then, as the storm eased and a gold white moon slid out from the scudding clouds, he woke.

Suddenly he emerged from the spell of the dream and remembered the day just gone. And the day to come when his father was planning to take Cockawun to town. Cockawun! Where was he now? Arthur looked up into the tree and saw a white glimmering in the moonlight. 'Cockawun,' he called coaxingly.

The white form glided down, down through the silhouette of branches and glittering rain-wet leaves. Down to the sodden earth where Arthur crouched. 'Cocky's a good boy,' he croaked, and Arthur felt tears coming from deep deep inside. Tears of loss from a grief too big to bear.

'I won't let Dad take you away,' he said

fiercely. 'You belong here with me. We're going to stay together all our lives.'

He rummaged in his pockets for the cheese. Cockawun loved cheese too, so they shared it. The potatoes were a soggy, sloppy mess. 'Fancy some mashed potato, Cocky?' Arthur grinned in the dark.

But Cockawun had had enough potatoes that day to last him a lifetime. He did not fancy any more. Arthur did not fancy them either. He wiped his fingers on some leaves and cuddled Cockawun to his chest.

Overhead the rain clouds were gathering again. Arthur emptied the water out of his boots. 'They'll overflow if I don't, with the downpour we'll get from this lot,' he observed to Cockawun. 'I reckon we'd better try to make ourselves a bit of a shelter.'

He looked at the stones. They'd make a wall or a fireplace.

But he could hear a voice in his head clearly saying, *'Don't touch the stones. Never touch the stones. The stones belong where they are. They must never be moved.'*

He looked up at the big tree with its bark

hanging in long strands. Perhaps he could weave a covering from them. But again he heard the voice. *'Don't touch the tree with an axe or fire. Never touch the tree.'*

So he left the bark ribbons weaving their own patterns in the wind and went out to scout beyond the stone circle. The storm had twisted several leafy branches off nearby trees and he dragged them back to the great tree. He patted its solid girth, taking comfort from its treeness, its roots going down down deep into the mysteries of the earth, its branches stretching up up to the everchanging sky, its leaves whispering the secrets of the winds.

The tree seemed to be offering him its shelter. So he made his little humpy, forcing the ends of the boughs as far into the earth as he could, leaning the leafy crowns against the tree trunk. He brought armfuls of bark to cover the ground inside, thinking as he did so of the armfuls of bracken he had carried to the fateful potato patch.

By now he was so cold and hungry he ate the potatoes he had brought, licking the mush from his fists and fingers. But it didn't satisfy. His stomach was clamouring for hot thick porridge with cream and golden syrup, and slabs of Mum's bread slathered with Mum's butter and jam.

He watched Cockawun foraging beyond the stones, finding food. Perhaps he could eat grubs like Cockawun. If only he had a fire to roast them. If only he had a fire . . .

But the only fire he had was burning within him. The fire of his anger against his father. The rage of betrayal. The desperate fury of determination to save Cockawun.

Storm

Arthur crawled into his shelter, pulling the bark around him, pretending it was the possum-skin rug from his bed at home. Home.

He drifted again into sodden sleep stained with dreams, and wakened to damp fingers of daylight seeping through the leaves, touching his aching cold. Home?

Was Dorothy doing her sums and her spelling at the kitchen table now? Was Ellie 'helping' her? Was his mother slicing onions and carrots into the big stockpot on the stove?

And his father? He would have had to bring in the cows. And clean up after milking. And fill the wood box. All by himself because Arthur had run away. Would his father go to town, now that Cockawun had gone? Or was he at this moment out looking for his right-hand helper?

Arthur stirred with fear. Fear for Cockawun. He began to shiver. Perhaps they hadn't gone far enough into the forest. He could not think how far they might have come yesterday. Distance and darkness and rain blurred his memory. Only the dreaming was clear. The men dancing, the boys, the singing, the flickering flaring firelight.

Oh, the fire ... The shivering aching fear and cold turned to fierce burning. The singing became shouting. Shrieking. Arthur struggled in the tangled bark. Cockawun. Where was Cockawun? 'Cockawun!' he called and his voice was wild and hoarse. 'Cockawun!'

Then he heard Cockawun's voice. Calling. Close. He saw Cockawun's black eyes staring at him. Black. Black.

'Cockawun,' he said and his voice was faint. With hunger and fear and fever. 'Cockawun, we'll always stay together. Unless you want to leave me. Unless you want to go back to the bush for ever and ever. You *can* be a wild bird,

Cockawun. You can be. We can be together in my dreams. Go now, Cockawun. Find Cockatoo and the others. Go! You must never be in a town. In a cage. On a chain.' Arthur's voice broke and he shuddered, closing his eyes, his mind, against the unthinkable pictures of a captive Cockawun.

Cockawun squatted on the boy's shoulder, gently nibbling him, gently lifting strands of his dripping hair. But Arthur did not respond. He was in another world, another time, a dream, a delirium. Cockawun hunched in beside him, making small sounds. But Arthur could hear only the old song, the singing that had come with the storm.

Even the great tree swayed and writhed in the roaring wind. Cockawun tucked in his head, waiting with the patience and wisdom of a wild creature. But the wind raged on. The rain drove in angry squalls, biting cold and hard. The boy moaned and twitched and suddenly called again, 'Cockawun!'

At once the bird was all alertness, cocking his head, staring at the boy with his dark unwinking eyes. He nibbled the boy's pale cheek, then his numb fingers. The boy sobbed. The bird moved to the opening of the crude little shelter. Outside, the ground was littered with leaves and bark, twigs and branches. The air was whirling with debris.

The bird lumbered out into the clearing and took off, wings beating heavily against the wind. It circled the tree twice, then disappeared among the tall timber. The boy called again from his dream, then lapsed into shuddering silence.

The darkness of the storm had already been swallowed by the darkness of the night when a loud 'Coo–eee!' came seeking through the trees encircling the clearing. Buffeted and broken though it was, it somehow pierced the darkness of the boy's sleep.

The cooeee came again. And again. The boy roused himself. Was it another dream? Was the gleam among the trees a lantern? Or was it the dream flame alive in the relentless rain?

And where was Cockawun? Arthur panicked. What had happened to Cockawun? He called his beloved bird. 'Cockawun!' The desperate cry rang through the clearing.

Suddenly Cockawun was beside him in the

shelter, tweaking his nose, tweaking his hair. Arthur knew then that he wasn't dreaming. That the voice was his father's. 'Arthur! Arthur! Where are you?'

He tried to stand up. But he couldn't. He tried to call. But he couldn't. Then he heard Cockawun answering for him. 'Cocky's a good boy. Cocky want a biscuit.'

The lantern came closer and closer until its light blinded Arthur. He shut his eyes and heard his father saying, 'Thank God I've found you. Thanks to Cockawun, too.'

'Hello, Dad,' Arthur whispered.

'Hello, son.' His father picked him up.

Arthur felt his dad's bristly face warm with wetness. But the rain was cold on his own. He felt the warm salt taste of his father's cheek. 'Sorry, Dad,' he whispered. 'I didn't mean to worry you and Mum.'

'It's all right, son. You're going home now.'

Arthur struggled in his father's arms. 'Cockawun,' he muttered. 'You won't send Cockawun away. Ever. Will you?'

'No. Never. I promise,' his father said.

Arthur lapsed into limp silence, dimly aware

of the strength of the arms carrying him, and the white shape that was Cockawun looking down at him from his father's shoulder.

There were hot bricks wrapped in newspaper in his bed at home, fire-warmed towels to rub his hair and cold shivering body, hot soup in a mug which his mother held to his lips. Then sleep. Sleep, dreamless sleep. With Dorothy's beloved teddy and Ellie's precious rag doll on his pillow beside him.

When he woke the rain had stopped. The sky was blue and the sun was shining. He could hear the cows down in the big paddock and the sound of his dad's axe in the forest. His sisters were reciting times-tables in the kitchen and his mother was at the chopping board. Rusty was whimpering in a possum dream by the bed, Snowy was curled up at Arthur's feet. All was as it should be.

But Cockawun? Where was Cockawun? Arthur sat up in bed and stared in astonishment. Cockawun was sitting on the back of a chair beside him. 'Cockawun,' he whispered. 'You're not supposed to be inside. Don't get me into more trouble,' he pleaded.

His mother heard him. She came in as he was trying to hide Cockawun under the possum-skin rug. 'It's all right, Arthur,' she said, pushing back his hair and feeling his forehead. 'It was Cockawun who came and told us you were in the forest and showed Dad where to find you. Without his help Dad might still have been looking.'

Arthur knew she was thinking that it could have been weeks before his dad had found him. They both knew how dense the bush was, how sheer the cliffs fell down into the gullies, how steeply the waterfall dashed against the rocks.

'Sorry, Mum,' Arthur said.

She ruffled his hair up into a crest. 'You and your bird,' she said. 'Well, a boy's got to have a mate, and it's a bit lonely at times up here by yourself, I know.' She brought cocoa in her best cup and thick slices of bread and golden honey that smelled of the bush, and sat on the end of his bed while he demolished them. For Cockawun there was a piece of bread and jam.

'It's true, isn't it, that Cockawun won't be sent away?' Arthur asked as he put down the cup in its gold-rimmed saucer.

'Yes, it's true, Arthur,' his mum said. 'He's one of the family now, forever. You gave him his chance to be a wild bird again. But he knows where he belongs.'

'And I know where I belong,' Arthur said. 'Dad can't work the cross-cut saw without me. It needs both of us for old Push-'im-'e-go—Pull-'im-'e-come.' He climbed out of bed, hurried into his dry clothes and set off with Cockawun to find his father.

Growing Up

As the sun was setting against rosy clouds, Arthur talked to his father in the cosiness of the cow bail, sweet with the scent of summer hay. 'Mum said Cockawun came and got you, and showed you where I was.' He needed to hear it from his father.

'That's right. He's a mischief-maker, but he cares about you. You know he took you to the bora ground. He took you along the ancient pathway of the Old People. He knew you'd be safe there. I always knew it was there. I was going to take you there myself one day, when you were older. It's a special place. And you must never touch the stones. Never.'

'Yes, Dad, I know.'

'Or the tree.'

'I know, Dad. They belong there. Like Cockawun belongs here.'

His father tousled his hair so that it stood up like Cockawun's crest. 'Now you're two of a kind,' he said. 'And our first job is to make a cage to keep the pumpkins in. I reckon Cockawun won't be beaten by that bit of wire you put on the latch of the shed door. He's not stupid and he never gives up.'

So the year went by. Arthur filled a big kerosene drum with plenty of manure and replanted the fragments of potato, then covered it with wire netting to keep Cockawun out. He helped Dorothy and Ellie to make a cubbyhouse near the pea patch, so they could watch over it while they played. It was a celebration when Arthur dug a bucketful of new potatoes and his sisters picked a basketful of peas. And Cockawun was given a biscuit.

The seasons passed. The lyrebirds in the forest added some of Cockawun's calls to their repertoire and sometimes Cockawun was tricked into answering back. A pair of eagles nested in the top of the tallest tallow wood and came back each year to rear another brood in the mighty tree. The brush turkeys built and rebuilt their mound in the bush each spring to incubate their eggs. And the notes of the bellbirds tinkled and rang through the trees.

The bees feasted in the fringed white blossoms of the brush box trees and filled the combs in the hives under the pear trees with the sweetest honey Arthur knew. Up on the hillside the spring never ran dry and down in the valley the water cascaded over the cliff in a shimmering lacy mist that always reminded Arthur of his mother in her wedding dress in the photo over the mantelpiece.

The koalas grunted and fought in the blue gums in the forest and occasionally came down to sleep in the trees at the edge of the clearing. The forty black chooks cackled and scratched and in one memorable week Dorothy and Ellie collected ninety-six eggs. The seventy-two Jersey cows grazed and calved and squirted out splendid quantities of rich creamy milk every day, morning and evening. Dorothy and Ellie learned from their mother how to make butter.

One winter, snow fell, hushing the bush and its creatures. In the home paddock, Arthur, Dorothy and Ellie built a snowman and made snowballs. But Cockawun huddled, puzzled and cold, in an apple tree. Snow fights were no fun for him.

Every spring the swallows came back and nested under the eaves along the verandah. Arthur cut a kerosene tin down and fixed it as a ledge underneath to catch the droppings.

Cockawun behaved himself. Mostly. He still got restless occasionally and followed the black cockatoos when he heard their wild calls, foraging for grubs with the yellow-tailed, feasting on glossy berries with the red-tailed. Arthur noticed that it was always after the white cockatoos had been around that Cockawun became mischievous. So then he was extra vigilant.

The trickiest time was always in the autumn when the persimmons began to ripen. Cockawun was very partial to persimmons. The problem was that Arthur's dad was, too, and if Cockawun took more than his fair share, Arthur's dad would start to mutter and rumble. Arthur tried netting the tree, but that was just a game for Cockawun, who shredded the net very quickly. Arthur tried hanging tin cans to discourage Cockawun. But that was another game. Then he built a persimmon cage, a cage for the tree. So Cockawun had to learn to ask for his persimmons. But he had the freedom of the sunflower patch, which Arthur planted each year for him. Sunflower seeds were his favourite food.

After Arthur had finished his school lessons at the kitchen table for ever, his dad bought a car. Arthur could already drive the old farm truck. But now he learned to drive his mother to town, because she often had to go to the doctor.

Arthur was sad about that. But glad in another way. Because he liked the receptionist in the doctor's office. Amy was her name. Arthur began to take her bunches of flowers from the bush. Once he even took Cockawun to town to meet Amy. She loved Cockawun at first sight and Cockawun looked from Arthur to her with his knowing black eyes and hopped onto her shoulder. Arthur grinned. There was no doubt that Cockawun understood a lot.

Then his mother had to go to hospital. For a long time. So Arthur drove his father down the winding road mile after mile through the forest to town every week. Until the doctor said his mother could come home. She liked lying out on the verandah in the sun, and Cockawun sat on the railing beside her.

The day came when Arthur had to help his father dig her grave out at the edge of the clearing where the bellbirds called while they buried her. Cockawun watched from a nearby tree and afterwards he did not speak again.

Dorothy and Ellie left home after their mother died. Dorothy began to train to be a nurse at the hospital in town. And Ellie went and boarded in town so she could go to school, because there was nobody left at home to teach her.

Arthur went away to the war, leaving Cockawun with his dad. With only Cockawun for company, Mr Wiseman began to grow fond of him. The old truce of years turned into friendship. Mr Wiseman used to talk about times gone by, about the forest, the farm, the children. And about his wife. Cockawun never spoke. But the way he listened, head on one side with such a wise look, was enough. And he danced and raised his crest and followed Mr Wiseman wherever he went. They were always together and Mr Wiseman was never lonely.

Arthur wrote letters to them whenever he could, and dreamed of the cool sweet bush and Amy. When the war was over and he came back, Cockawun began to speak again.

Arthur married Amy, who came up to the farm to live, and soon there were nappies blowing on the line again. But Cockawun never unpegged them or nipped the flowers off the roses Amy planted along the verandah. He watched over the children as faithfully as Rusty Three, and one early spring day shrieked till Arthur came when a snake emerged from under a log where Jim, Louise and Helen were playing.

Louise and Helen loved the bowerbirds as much as their aunties had done. They looked for parrot feathers in the bush and left them near the bower. They planted cornflowers and delphiniums so that the bowerbirds had blue flowers to pick. Sometimes Cockawun picked the flowers for them, but he always left them on the ground where they could find them.

Jim wasn't so interested in the bush and its

creatures. He preferred to spend his time fiddling with machinery in the shed. Arthur was sorry Jim didn't care about the bush as he did, but he was glad Jim took an interest in these other things.

One stormy day Arthur had to dig a second grave beside the first. Cockawun rode on his shoulder as he carried his father's body, light now and shrunken with age, to lay it to rest beside his mother's. When Cockawun called and flew off into the forest, Arthur followed.

Cockawun flew and Arthur walked. Cockawun perched and Arthur caught up. For hours it seemed as if Cockawun was weaving their way through the tall tallow woods and the pink-stemmed brush box trees. Suddenly Arthur realised where they were going.

The great old tree was towering before him. It had outlived generations of boys become men, generations of cockatoos, black and white. It stood triumphant in its treeness, its majesty, the pattern of its leaf shadows flickering across the sunlit clearing like half-remembered dreams.

The stones lay there silent still, old in their circle, even older in themselves. Out of the earth before humans existed. And the voice in Arthur's head was clear. '*Never touch the stones. The stones must remain.*'

Memories flooded through Arthur. He was a little boy again, frightened, lonely, cold, oh, so cold. And wet. Drenched to the skin. Men were dancing and boys became men. Then he felt again the strength of his father's arms, the tenderness of his mother's touch.

Tears deeper than Arthur had known for a very long time came burning up from within as he leaned against the tree. Hot, cleansing, healing tears, which Cockawun watched as he sat on a branch above Arthur's head. At last he flew down to Arthur's shoulder and nibbled gently at his cheek. 'Cocky's a good boy,' he said softly.

'Cocky certainly is,' Arthur said. 'And Cocky knows a thing or two.' He scratched Cockawun's head fondly. Together they went back home through the wild green bush, breathing its aromatic air, pulsing with its past.

One day he would bring his children here.

Hero

The next summer Arthur packed up all the family in the old truck and took them to the beach. It was their first holiday. They pitched Arthur's father's old canvas tent in the tea-tree, and hung the food safe from a bough. Cocka-wun explored excitedly, calling loudly as he circled over the strange bush.

He flew after the children as they ran through the sandhills down onto the beach, and circled over them as they splashed into the breaking waves at the water's edge. He fossicked through the foam ribbons at the tide line, bursting the big bright bubbles with squawks of delight.

Then he found the seaweed, bunch after tempting bunch of sea-grapes just waiting to be pecked with satisfying pops. He was busy for hours while the children dug channels, built castles and walls, and buried each other up to their chins in the sand.

Other children and their parents came down to look at the big white bird that was not a seagull. 'It's a cocky!' 'Hello, Cocky!' 'Pretty Cocky.'

Cockawun bowed and raised his bright-yellow crest. He spread his wide white wings and swayed from side to side. He loved having all the people around him in a circle watching.

'Dance, Cocky, dance!' a boy called.

So Cockawun danced. Danced and danced on the shining gold sand while the great green waves with their white crests rolled in from the ocean.

Every day Cockawun danced for the people on the beach. They brought him biscuits and even a cob of corn. He perched on top of umbrellas and nibbled at their metal rings. He investigated picnic baskets and thermos flasks, soft-drink bottles and even ladies' handbags. He was everybody's favourite and he loved it.

'You're a show-off, Cockawun,' Arthur told him. But he enjoyed Cockawun's popularity, too. It was a holiday everyone would talk about for a long time.

Then late on the afternoon before they were leaving, Cockawun became a hero. A boy who had ventured out beyond his depth found he couldn't swim back against the pull of the waves. Nobody noticed. Nobody except Cockawun. When *his* family were in the water he always patrolled the shallows, flying up and down with strong steady wing beats.

He saw the boy out beyond the others. He heard his faint cry. He saw him disappear under the curling breaker and bob up again as helpless as a rag doll. Swiftly he flew to where the boy was gasping and struggling. He circled the boy, shrieking at the top of his raucous voice. Shrieking, shrieking above the sounds of the waves and the calls of the children at play.

Arthur, dozing on the warm sand, heard Cockawun's note. He shaded his eyes and searched the sky to see Cockawun gleaming white out over the breakers. 'Stay there, Cockawun! I'm coming!' he yelled.

He raced down the beach, seized a surfboard lying at the water's edge, and set off towards Cockawun, paddling with all his strength. He was not a good swimmer, but he was strong. And Cockawun's shouts called him on. He pulled the choking terrified boy onto the board and turned back to shore. Cockawun flew ahead, calling triumphantly.

Willing hands were waiting to help Arthur and the boy in over the last stretch. Towels were waiting to dry them. People were eager to pat Arthur on the shoulder, to congratulate him, to thank him for rescuing the boy. But Arthur shrugged his shoulders. 'It was Cockawun,' he said. 'He gave the alarm. It's Cockawun you ought to be thanking.'

Again Cockawun found himself in the centre of an admiring circle. He danced and squawked and announced, 'Cocky's a good boy!' while everyone cheered and clapped. Then he rode back to the tent in triumph on Arthur's shoulder. Jim, Louise and Helen hugged their father. Arthur tousled their salty hair, ruffling it into crests. 'It might have been one of you,' he said gruffly. Their mother nodded solemnly.

Next morning when the boy's grateful family came looking for Arthur and Cockawun, they were disappointed to find the rescuers had already gone home. 'I'm really sorry not to have thanked them again and found out who they were. But we'll never forget that pair, will we?' the boy's mother said to her husband.

For two more years Arthur took the family back to the beach for summer holidays. Cockawun was a favourite with the campers, even though he sometimes teased their dogs or raided their food boxes. Everyone remembered or was told the story of how he had saved the drowning boy. The boy's family, who also returned, came and spoke to them on the beach, and the boy Jack, who had grown quite a bit taller, often played with Jim, Louise and Helen, and took Cockawun for rides on his bike, even though Cockawun liked to unscrew the tyre valves.

The two families met up again at the beach in the third summer. But then they lost touch. At the beginning of the fourth summer Arthur's wife fell ill. She had to stay in hospital in the town and the doctors told Arthur that even when she was better, from now on she would have to visit hospital for treatment three times a week for the rest of her life. Arthur drove home up the mountain with a heavy heart.

The road was better now than it had been when they used to drive down and up while his mother was in hospital. But it was steep and treacherous still, with mud slides and washaways, crumbling edges and sometimes trees smashed down across it by the wind.

After Arthur had milked the cows and fed the children, he and Cockawun went out into the bush. Even in the dark Arthur knew where Cockawun was leading him. Along the ancient trail trodden by so many feet. Bare feet, brown feet. Feet which knew frost on grass and sun on rocks. Feet which knew thorns and stinging plants, mud and running water.

Overhead the sky was so clear it seemed as if the stars were glittering in the treetops. Arthur took deep breaths of the sweet still night air, listening to the night sounds he knew so well, the rustlings, the squeakings, the soft hoot of an owl and the mournful call of the mopoke.

They reached the clearing, the meeting place where men had gathered and boys became men, where the silent stones lay in waiting, guardians of the wisdom of untold generations. For the third time Arthur leaned against the great tree and felt its grace and its strength flowing into him.

If he had to leave this place, then it was so.

Memories danced around him, flickering dimly, flaring brightly. Memories of his father. Memories of his mother. Memories of the farm, the bush. His childhood, his boyhood, here in this beloved place. He groaned with the pain of the thought of leaving it. This land which had been home for all but ten years of his life.

Then there were memories of Amy, who although a town girl, had never once complained about the rough lonely life here in the bush, so far away from her family and friends and all the things she had known and grown up with. She had given all that up for him. Now it was his turn to show his love for her. He must give up all this for her. And never never utter one word of his pain and loss.

Silently he embraced the great tree for the last time. Silently he walked around the stone circle, which seemed to glow in the starlight. Silently the tears flowed down his weather-beaten cheeks. In the distance a mopoke called, and Arthur knew it was time to go.

Shot!

Arthur found a little house near the hospital. It was near the school, too.

Amy said, 'Arthur, you mustn't give up the farm because of me. You love it too much. It's the only life you've ever known. What will you do?'

Arthur said sturdily, 'Nobody will want to buy the farm. But I can sell the stock. Then I'll find a job. You'll see. With a regular weekly wage. No more getting up in the dark and the cold for the cows. No more worrying because the frost's got the pumpkins or the hail's ruined the apples. Or the bandicoots have eaten the potatoes. Or the sheep have been flyblown.

'We'll be able to go to the shops like everyone else and buy our food. And it's time the children went to school and got a better education than I had. I do believe young Jim won't want to carry on the farm. His heart was never in it like mine was at his age. He's more interested in machinery and things. This way he can become an apprentice and learn a good trade.'

Amy stroked his hair, which had begun to grey over the last month. 'What about Cockawun?' she said. 'Surely he'll fret?'

'Then he'll just have to learn, like the rest of us,' Arthur said, pushing back memories of the day long ago when his father had threatened to condemn Cockawun to a life sentence of town.

Arthur found a job as a caretaker at the hospital. He kept the lawns neat and the gardens cheerful with flowers. He carried cases for frail patients, and babies for new mothers going home. And Cockawun often went with him.

Cockawun was a favourite with patients and the staff liked him, too, because he gave everyone something to smile about. He danced and displayed and gave chat and cheek to anyone who talked to him, from the matron down.

But he was not a favourite in the street where he now lived. His raucous responses to the noises of the town were not appreciated by the neighbours.

At first he had something to say about every car and truck that passed. Then after a few months not even a motorbike would excite him. But he never missed the sound of the ambulance or the fire engine.

And he was intrigued by the telephone and screeched, 'Answer that phone! Answer that phone!' until someone did. He could hear a plane before people knew that it was coming and he would call and call, 'Plane's coming! Plane's coming!' until it had passed over, while the occasional helicopter sent him into a frenzy of squawking and shouting, 'Chopper! Chopper!'

Soon the neighbours were complaining, even threatening. Arthur was worried and didn't know what to do. So he hung his father's old fob watch on the verandah. Cockawun loved it and would sit by the hour, head cocked, listening to its quiet tick, just giving a mutter of enjoyment from time to time.

He had another favourite place and pastime,

too. He loved to sit in the macadamia tree by the fence, chewing the tough-shelled nuts to extract their crisp round kernels. But the neighbour over the fence had a smoker's cough which came on suddenly and kept him spluttering and coughing for minutes. When Cockawun heard the rasping noise starting, he would drop his nut and shriek, 'Quit the cigarettes, man, quit the cigarettes!'

Arthur laughed when he heard Cockawun the first time. But the neighbour was not amused. It was bad enough having his wife nagging, without the wretched bird next-door imitating her. He became irate at Cockawun's chorus each time he had a coughing fit, and one day he lost all patience.

He fetched his gun and took aim, hitting Cockawun square in the left eye.

Arthur heard the shot, heard Cockawun screaming. He ran out and saw the neighbour hastening inside with his gun. The blood was staining Cockawun's white cheek. 'You beast! You miserable beast!' Arthur shouted after the neighbour. But it was more important to see to Cockawun.

He hurried him to the vet, who said, 'I can't save the eye. But lucky it wasn't his brain. He's still got one good eye and he'll live to be a hundred yet.'

Arthur spent all his spare time the next week building a new fence along the boundary. A high fence, too high for anyone to see over. And he planted some roses, thorny, prickly climbing roses all along it. 'Stay with the nuts,' he urged Cockawun. 'His cough is his business if he's silly enough to smoke. And don't you dare sit on this fence or give him advice, ever.'

Cockawun cocked his head, listening. He often went back to the macadamia tree, but he never ventured onto the fence and he never again took any notice of the cough beyond.

Amy grew thinner and paler, and one day she went to hospital, never to come home again. She was buried in the town cemetery beside her parents among rows of engraved stones. Cockawun went to the funeral with Arthur and the children, and didn't make a sound. But he nibbled Arthur's ear and stroked his cheek, tasting again the salt of tears.

One day that spring they drove up the

mountain to the farm. The swallows were already nesting under the eaves and the apple trees were pink with blossom, humming with bees. 'Good honey there,' Arthur said.

But Jim said, 'It's easier to buy it. No stings. No mess. Remember how you used to have to strain it, and all the bother it was in the kitchen? Not for me. In fact the farm's not for me, Dad. You ought to sell it. It's only going to rack and ruin.'

Cockawun saw Arthur's shoulders sagging. He picked a spray of wild bluebells from the grass and brought it to Arthur. 'Cocky's a good boy,' he said, raising his crest. Arthur ruffled it fondly. 'Yes, Cocky, you are.'

They walked to the spot where the bowerbird had its playground, and Arthur laid the delicate little flowers on the edge of the bower. Just then a flock of white cockatoos swept overhead, calling, calling.

Cockawun took to the air. 'Cockawun, Cockawun.' His yearning cry echoed through the bush and his gleaming white form grew smaller, ever smaller in the distance until he disappeared.

Arthur's heart was pounding as he stood waiting. The scent of wattle wafted to him, the chink of bellbirds tinkled through the trees. A wallaby bounded through the bush and a blue wren twittered and bounced on a blackberry bramble.

'Blackberries,' Arthur growled. He fetched a fern hook from the shed and slashed and sweated hour after hour, waiting for Cockawun's return.

The air grew cooler, the sun began to slip behind the purple mountains, the bees fell silent, the daisies in the grass closed their petals.

'Come on, Dad. What are we waiting for? Cockawun's gone bush. Let's get going. I'm taking my girlfriend to the pictures tonight. It's a rotten road at the best of times and I'm in a hurry now.'

Arthur climbed into the car slowly and drove out through the gate. He stopped, waiting for Jim to hop out and close it.

But Jim said, 'What's the use? It's half off its hinges now anyway. Let's get going.'

Arthur didn't look back. He kept his eyes on the winding dirt road, skirting patches of slurry,

hugging the inner bend near washaways, sound-
ing the horn at corners. Not speaking, but
listening, straining his ears for the sound of
cockatoos. Wishing with all his heart that his
hearing was as good as theirs.

New Friends

Cockawun did not come back and Arthur was silent with sadness, tense with listening. Neighbours called in. 'What's happened to your cocky? He was a noisy wretch but we kind of miss him now he's gone. No one to tell us that a plane is coming or an ambulance is on its way.'

The neighbour who had shot at Cockawun spoke to Arthur through the fence one day. 'What's happened to that dratted bird of yours? Someone give him a poison bait?'

Arthur didn't reply. Couldn't reply. How could you explain the taste of freedom to someone who could only think in terms of poison bait?

Jim got the apprenticeship Arthur had always thought he would and left home. One by one the girls also left, to study in the city. Louise wanted to be a librarian, Helen a teacher. Arthur was proud of them, but he missed them.

He was alone with his books and his photos and his memories. He still went to work at the hospital, but his heart was not in it any more. So many memories there, too. Bringing Amy down from the mountain three times to have their babies. Taking her home with them. Bringing her back again. Time and again. Until it was the last time. He grew to hate the sound of ambulances. And helicopters. And telephones. And planes.

One Friday night he decided he would give up his job and go back to the farm. Away from all the noise. Back to the sounds of the bush. He would tell the matron on Monday.

He packed up his swag and drove to the coast, to the beach where they used to camp. There were houses there now with gardens, instead of shacks in the bush, and the sandy tracks had become metalled roads. There were kiosks and shops and even a supermarket. But still there was the smell of the sea and the sound of the breakers on the long golden beach.

Arthur found a patch of tea-tree and slung a canvas fly between two big bushes. He boiled his billy and grilled his sausages. He walked along the beach in the moonlight, gazing on the silver pathway stretching to the horizon, gathering a bunch of sea-grapes from the tide wrack. He smiled, remembering Cockawun nipping his way through bunch after bunch.

He slept peacefully for the first time since Cockawun had gone off, lulled by the sound of the sea and the wind in the casuarinas. The next day he walked on the beach again and watched children feeding seagulls.

'Hi,' a boy said. 'Isn't this a great place? Have you been here before? We come every year. My uncle reckons he was rescued from drowning here once by a white cockatoo. What do you think of that for a story?'

'I'm glad he remembers,' Arthur said. 'I knew that cockatoo. He called me to your uncle and together we brought him in.'

'Pull the other one,' the boy said. 'You're as bad as my uncle. You think us kids will swallow anything. Cockies don't ever come to the beach.'

'That one did,' Arthur said. 'He always came everywhere with us. We were camping in the tea-trees.'

'Where is he now?' the boy demanded.

Arthur bit his lips as if that would stop the lump in his throat, the tears in his eyes.

The boy looked at him. 'He's dead, is he?'

Arthur shook his head and a betraying tear fell free.

The boy looked concerned. 'I'm sorry. I believe you. I really do. Let's hear the story from you.'

They sat together on a foreshore seat. The boy offered Arthur a piece of bubblegum and gave a demonstration. Arthur laughed. 'Cockawun would have liked that.'

'Was that his name?'

Arthur nodded. 'He had a sister. At least we always said she was a sister. We called her Cock-atoo. My uncle rescued them from a big gum tree that was cut down to make way for Parliament House when it was being built in Canberra.'

'What?' said the boy. 'The new Parliament House that's like a funny sort of pyramid? I've been there. But that's been built since my uncle grew up.'

'No, not that one,' Arthur explained. 'The first one, when Canberra was being built, too. You see, Canberra just used to be a farm with paddocks and sheep and gum trees. And before that, of course, Aborigines lived there.'

'It's not like that now,' the boy said. 'There's the Mint where they make the money, and the Art Gallery and the National Library and the lake with the water jet and the carillon. I've been there with my family. We went last holidays.'

'Funny,' Arthur said. 'I've never been there.'

'You ought to go sometime,' the boy said. 'Everyone should see Canberra. I did a project on it for school. Got an A for it.'

'Well done,' Arthur said. He knew from his children what a lot of work went into projects.

'Yep,' the boy said. 'And I like writing stories. Tell me about Cockawun. We have to write a story about the holidays when we go back to school.'

So Arthur told him how his uncle had

brought home the two baby cockies and how they had reared them from naked fledglings. He told how his father had bought the farm up on the mountains and the boy gazed up to the dark, blue ranges in the distance. 'Right up there?'

'Right up there,' Arthur nodded.

'What did you do for electricity and TV and all that?'

'Didn't have any,' Arthur said. 'Kerosene lamps and candles, and a wood stove that Mum made beautiful bread and scones in. And a meat safe in a gum tree. And sing-songs at night when we weren't watching stars or hunting possums.'

The boy whistled a long low whistle of ad- miration. 'Whew! Wait till I write about this at school! You were PIONEERS!' And his voice went high on the last word.

'We-ell,' Arthur said. 'It wasn't as tough as that. Dad had a truck and Mum had a sewing machine. We kids used to treadle it for her.'

'So that was high-tech in your day?'

'Yes, you could put it that way, I guess. On our place, anyway.'

'And how did Cockawun and Cockatoo like

the bush?' The boy was full of questions, bright with curiosity.

But Arthur was silent before he could answer this one. How could he begin to describe the spell of the bush to this city kid who knew nothing of its scents, its secret sounds, its mystery and tiny treasures, many never to be seen by human eyes?

The boy nudged him. 'I thought you'd gone to sleep. My Grandpa does sometimes.'

'No. Just remembering,' Arthur said. As if he didn't remember every day. 'Well, Cockatoo went off with a flock of wild cockatoos one day. She never came back. That was all right. That was her choice. But Cockawun ...' Arthur paused again. 'Well, he thought he was one of the family. He was always about, getting into mischief, teasing the dog, the cat, annoying my father and mother. But he saved my little sister from a snake one day, and me when I was lost in the bush overnight.'

The boy's eyes were wide. 'Wow! This is some story! But where is he now?'

'We had to go and live in town. Someone shot at him for making so much noise. Then he went off one day when we went back to visit the farm. He saw the wild cockatoos and went off. I guess he was restless for his own. Every time a flock of wild cockatoos came over the mountain he'd get into extra mischief after they'd gone.'

The boy was silent for a while. He'd forgotten to blow his bubblegum for quite a time. Now he took it out of his mouth. 'Gee,' he said. 'I'm sorry. But I reckon he'll come back. I reckon he's missing you more than the bush and his wild friends. You're his best friend for life and cockies live till they're a hundred, don't they?'

Arthur nodded, strangely comforted by this boy whose uncle he and Cockawun had rescued on a long-ago summer day. He brightened with an idea. 'I'd like to meet Jack again after all these years. You look a bit like he did in those days. Perhaps you and your uncle would like to come up to the farm one day. Before you go home to the city?'

'That'd be great!' the boy exclaimed. 'Could we go tomorrow? Uncle's coming up from Sydney tomorrow to take us all home on Monday. Back to school, you know. I'll ask him. Wowee!

Won't he be surprised to know I've met the man who saved his life! He's never forgotten you. He's always hoped he'd meet you and Cocky again one day. He looks for you here every summer.'

Arthur was boiling his billy and grilling his fish over his camp fire that night, when a tall man came through the tea-trees with the boy. He put his hand out to Arthur. 'I'm Jack. I always hoped I'd meet you again one day. In fact I used to dream of it. Thank you for saving my life. I haven't wasted it. And young George here says you've invited us up to see your farm tomorrow. We'd love to come, wouldn't we, George?'

The boy's eyes were shining.

'George,' Arthur said slowly. 'My father's name was George.' It seemed as if the years were rolling back.

'Why don't we go in my four-wheel drive?' the boy-turned-man was saying. 'It looks as if it might be quite a road up the mountains. And I don't get a chance like that too often, to put it through its paces. Not in the city.'

'No, you wouldn't,' Arthur agreed, remembering his first trip to the Bulga when he was George's age.

Coming Home

Early next morning they drove in convoy to Arthur's house, where he left his truck.

'Don't worry about lunch,' Jack said. 'We've brought a barbecue.'

Arthur smiled. 'We used to call them chop picnics when I was George's age.' He put his swag in the house and locked the door behind him. He was about to climb into the 4WD when he suddenly made an excuse and returned to the verandah. He took a couple of blue pegs from the line and put them in his trouser pocket. Then he went into the kitchen and quickly opening the tin on the shelf, slipped a couple of biscuits into his shirt pocket.

All the way up the mountainside George was noticing things, asking questions. Arthur's eyes were searching the bush, scanning the horizon while he answered. But he would not admit, even to himself, what he longed to see. That gleam of white, that flash of yellow. The 4WD made easy work of the steep gradients and sharp curves. It flew through the mud slurries and the wet patches on the road.

'My ears are funny!' George exclaimed.

'We-ell,' said Arthur. 'You're up in the Bulga now. It's high up here. But your ears'll get used to it. They'd better. There's lots of sounds to hear, as well as things to see. And we're nearly there now.'

They swung in through the open gate and drove across the tussocky grass where a pair of startled wallabies leapt up in front of them, past the cow yards where the lichen was hanging in hairy green tassels from the timber rails, past the apple trees where king parrots and crimson rosellas were feasting. The 4WD pulled up by the pear tree and Arthur could not stop himself looking up hopefully into its yellowing leaves.

They got out and walked over to the house. One of the steps had rotted away, the verandah was sagging and the roof was full of holes. Arthur remembered the hole Cockawun had made over the kitchen door. He looked up. His patch was still there. He smiled and pushed open the door. There were dead leaves on the floor. Possums had nested in the chimney and there was the strong eucalyptus smell of their urine.

Arthur was embarrassed. What would his visitors think?

But George was ecstatic. 'So that was where your mother baked the bread! And that little corner room on the verandah. Was that yours? I wish I could sleep there.'

Jack was looking about with interest. 'This place has really got something. You can feel it as soon as you walk in. Some houses are like that. Not all. But this is special.'

They roamed about outside, exploring the dairy and the sheds, tracing the overgrown garden beds. Arthur found a sprig of forget-me-not. 'Come with me,' he said. They walked across the paddocks to the edge of the bush. Even George was quiet.

'Ever seen a bowerbird's playground?' Arthur asked. The city man and the city boy shook their heads. Arthur showed them and laid the forget-me-not at the edge of the display ground. 'They just love blue, you see,' he explained, taking the blue clothes pegs from his trouser pocket.

Jack fished in his pocket and took out a blue ballpoint pen. George said, 'We've got blue straws with our drink cans. They can have those, too.'

They'd finished their barbecue and drained their drink cans dry. Jack was still looking at the house, taking in the details of the rusty tank and broken-down pipes. George was examining droppings by the old vegetable patch.

'Wombat,' Arthur said. 'You can always tell the wombat by the shape. And they like to do it on a stone or a tussock, somewhere obvious. Marks their territory, you see.'

The boy was so interested in everything, so excited by each new discovery. Arthur's heart was warmed. He wondered whether to show the boy and his uncle the ancient pathway, the circle of stones. But it was getting late for the drive down the mountain, even in a 4WD. And somehow, Arthur felt in his bones, they'd be back. There would be time enough for that when the boy was older.

A flock of black cockatoos flapped over, uttering their eerie cry. 'Yellow-tails,' Arthur said. 'They go after the grubs in the gum trees and the wattles.'

'They're beautiful,' George said. 'Are they the guardians of the Bulga?'

Arthur looked at him approvingly. The boy had the spirit of the place.

'Yes,' he said. 'Them and the red-tails. They both love the tall timber on the ridge.'

'What about the white ones?'

'You don't see them so often,' Arthur said, wishing he could see them now. 'They tend to go off down the valley, down on the plains where it's been cleared more.'

At that moment he heard them calling, their raucous shrieks like no other. He watched eagerly, anxiously, the direction from which the calls were coming, closer and closer. Until the white shapes wheeled into view. Seven of them.

Could it be Cockatoo with her wild friends?
Could it be Cockawun?

Arthur's eyes ached with watching, his mouth was dry with expectation.

Suddenly one bird broke away from the flock and circled. It screamed and screamed again. And flew in to land on Arthur's shoulder.

George and Jack stood by in wonder. Nobody spoke.

Then Cockawun said, 'Cocky's a good boy. Cocky like a biscuit?'

Arthur fumbled in his shirt pocket. He produced a biscuit, then stroked Cockawun behind his crest. Cockawun raised it in delight and began to dance.

George exploded with excitement. 'Wait till I tell my teacher this! She won't believe it!'

'She'll have to,' his Uncle Jack said. 'I'll get it on video.' He went to the 4WD and got his camera.

'I think I could do with a cuppa tea,' Arthur said. 'So get some sticks, young George, and we'll boil the billy. And put some gumleaves on the fire. Smells good.'

They sat round on old lichened logs drinking

black tea with sugar out of chipped enamel mugs, and George thought he had never tasted anything so good. Cocky was putting on a real performance on the remains of the verandah rail and Jack was making sketches in a little notebook.

Suddenly Jack said, 'I don't know what you'd think of this idea. Tell me I've got a cheek and I'll shut up and never mention it again. But I'm an architect and I've dreamed about a place like this for years. Obviously it needs a bit of doing up and someone living here to keep an eye on things, possums out of the chimney and all that. Would you consider selling it to me, Arthur, and coming back yourself as caretaker?

'Then George and I could come up here for weekends and holidays and get to know it better. And you could show us. I realise this is a special place. I could feel it as soon as we came in the gate.'

Arthur looked at Jack and then at George. Their eyes were alight. His heart flared with new hopes, new dreams, new warmth. 'Sounds a great idea to me,' he said. 'When can we start fixing it up?'

Canberra

By the time the next holidays came around, Arthur was back up the Bulga, ensconced once more in his old home. When George came to stay, he brought his project of Canberra to show Arthur. 'You've got to go to Canberra,' he urged. Everyone's got to see Canberra at least once in their life. And you ought to take Cockawun. He must see the place where he was born.'

After George and Jack had gone back to Sydney, Arthur kept thinking about the boy's eager advice. 'What do you think, Cockawun?' he asked. 'Shall we go?'

Cockawun nodded his head and raised his yellow crest. 'Cocky's a good boy,' he said in his most ingratiating manner.

So Arthur went to town to make arrangements. He thought at first of flying. He'd never been in an aeroplane in his life. Flying was no novelty to Cockawun. So it was time he caught up. But when he found out that Cockawun would have to go in a pet pack, as freight, he gave up the idea of travelling by plane.

He looked at his old truck. It mightn't make the distance. So he enquired about the buses and he enquired about the train. He rather liked the idea of going by train. After all, he'd come to the Bulga by train. But he didn't want Cockawun in a box like last time. Cockawun would not like that. Not one little bit.

He rolled his swag and packed his bag, went to the station and bought his ticket for the train. But when the stationmaster saw Cockawun, he said, 'Pets not allowed with passengers. He'll have to go in the luggage van. And in a cage.'

'No cage,' Arthur said, 'and I want to travel with him. We're mates and he'd fret without me.' He didn't say that Cockawun might start investigating parcels in the van if he were on his own.

The stationmaster demurred and looked again at Arthur and Cockawun. Cockawun began to dance. 'Cocky's a good boy,' he announced.

'Okay then,' the stationmaster said. 'Just this once. No cage if you travel together in the luggage van. But no trouble either, or it'll be double trouble, with me in it, too.'

So Arthur and Cockawun travelled in the van. The guard was a friendly fellow, quite pleased to have a change in his usual routine. He scratched Cockawun's head and Cockawun danced and did all his tricks.

'I'll see you right in Sydney,' the guard told Arthur. 'Not every guard will take a passenger in his van, but I've got friends. We'll get you there.'

The train swayed and rocked and Cockawun swayed and rocked with it, ecstatic with the motion, while Arthur sat on his swag and yarned with the guard. In Sydney the guard made sure they got in the van of the train going to Canberra and waved them goodbye.

At last the long journey ended. Arthur was

sorry he hadn't seen anything of the countryside from the closed van, but that was a small sacrifice for the sake of having Cockawun arrive with dignity and in good spirits. As Arthur walked out of the station with Cockawun on his shoulder, people stared. Canberra received more than its share of unusual visitors, but this pair was more unusual than most.

Arthur looked for somewhere to stay, but the first two places both had signs up outside, NO PETS ALLOWED. He walked on, looking at a list he had collected at the station. There was a place called 'Treetops' that appealed to him. Surely they would have a sign up saying PETS WELCOME, ESPECIALLY BIRDS.

There was no sign but there were trees. Arthur felt encouraged and walked in. The woman at the reception desk looked at his swag, then noticed Cockawun. Her eyebrows went up but she smiled. Before Arthur could ask for a room she said, 'I'm sorry, sir, pets are not allowed here. And I think you'll find it's the same everywhere.'

Arthur felt deflated. Nonplussed. But not for long. 'There's got to be somewhere a fellow can camp,' he said. 'Perhaps you'd be kind enough to tell me where and how to find it.'

The woman smiled at him again. She liked this bushman, so different from the usual guests. 'Better still,' she said, 'I'll take you there. It's not out of my way home. I'm afraid I'll have to ask you to wait outside for half an hour until I leave. But I'll bring you a cup of tea.'

Arthur and Cockawun sat outside enjoying the late afternoon sun and fresh air after being closed up in luggage vans all day. Cockawun did a few circuits of the trees. 'Don't you go off now exploring, Cockawun. We're doing that together, you and I, in the morning.'

The woman brought the cup of tea and two biscuits. 'One for Cocky,' she explained. Cockawun swooped down and sat on the back of a terrace chair. 'Ta,' he said. 'Cocky's a good boy.' And he danced his thanks.

At the camping ground there were signs that said NO DOGS and NO CATS. But there wasn't one that said NO COCKATOOS. The manager looked at Cockawun. 'Well,' he said. 'You're not a dog and you're not a cat, and there's nothing in the regulations about you. So I guess you can stay.' He looked doubtfully at Arthur. 'But I don't know about letting him stay in one of our cabins.'

'No problem,' said Arthur. 'Under the stars suits us fine.'

The manager still looked a bit doubtful. 'I hope you're not an early bird,' he said sternly to Cockawun, who assured him he was a good boy. 'Well, no mischief then. No sneaking into other peoples' tents and interfering with their things. And the first complaint I get about a tent peg being pulled out, you're out, too. And I mean *out*.'

Cockawun put on his butter-wouldn't-melt-in-his-beak look and Arthur hastened to reassure the manager. 'He's nearly seventy now and I'm past that. I think we know how to behave.'

'Well, I hope so,' the manager said. 'But my grandfather had a cocky just like that and it was always getting into mischief.'

'I'll keep an eye on him,' Arthur promised.

Celebrity

Next morning Arthur decided to walk to the new Parliament House and look on the way for all the landmarks young George had mentioned. People in cars slowed down as they passed him and Cockawun, but Arthur did not mind. 'Let them stare. It's not every day they get the chance to see one of the inhabitants of the first Parliament House in Australia,' he told Cockawun, who waltzed with excitement at the pride in Arthur's voice.

It was a long way, but Cockawun took to the air frequently, doing little sorties of his own, exploring this new old territory. Several drivers stopped and offered Arthur a lift, but he declined politely. It was a beautiful sunny day and he wanted to savour every moment of it.

It was quite a climb up to new Parliament House. Its great flag stood out in the wind against the blue sky and its green lawns looked like velvet carpets unrolled down the slopes. There were buses with interstate numberplates drawn up in the car park, and many cars, and a crowd of tourists was gathered outside the entrance of the huge building. Cockawun did a circuit of the great flagpole then swooped in over the crowd.

A boy in a party of school children shouted, 'Look! A cocky!' Cockawun swept low over the heads of the astonished tourists and landed with practised precision on Arthur's shoulder.

'Wow, did you see that?' people said to each other. Boys and girls clapped and whistled in approval. Even adults cheered. Arthur actually blushed with everyone staring at him. But Cockawun was in his element.

'Cocky's a good boy,' he announced and began his routine of crest raising, wing flapping, swaying and dancing. The more the crowd laughed and roared, the more Cockawun performed. There was no stopping him. And the crowd wanted more. The queue that had formed to enter the building broke up.

'This is better than polly-watching any day,' one man said to his wife.

Cockawun's acute hearing picked up the remark. 'Pretty Polly,' he said, flirting his crest and doing a little number. The crowd clapped.

'A rumba! A rumba, and Pretty Polly can lead us,' a girl called.

In a moment the line had re-formed, but not progressing in the direction of the entrance. The girl grabbed Arthur by the hand and started the dancing. People were singing and the few who did not join in were clapping and beating time. The line wriggled round the forecourt with its inlaid Aboriginal designs and was about to start a second circle when two police officers stepped in.

'Okay, Okay. You've had your fun,' they said good-humouredly. 'Break it up now and go on inside for what you came to see.'

But suddenly everyone was reaching for their camera or their video recorder, and the flashes and whirrings excited Cockawun even more. He took off and circled the crowd to their delight.

'He's yours, is he?' one of the police officers asked Arthur.

'I wouldn't say he was mine,' Arthur said. 'More like, I'm his. He was born here in a tree that was cut down to make way for the first Parliament House. And I've brought him back to find his roots.'

Those nearest to Arthur in the crowd chuckled at the old bushman's dry wit and passed the story on.

Arthur turned to go towards the entrance. But one of the police officers stopped him. 'Not that way, sir.'

'But we want to see Parliament House,' Arthur said.

'Sorry, sir, but livestock are not permitted in the building.'

A woman beside Arthur said, 'What about all the galahs in there already? Why can't the cocky see his relations?'

The people around laughed and cheered, and the word went back through the crowd. 'They won't let the old fella and the cocky in.' Then everyone began to boo and hiss.

'It's a shame. It's a downright shame,' the woman told the officer. 'You can see the man has come a long way. And it's our Parliament House as much as those galahs' inside. After all, we paid for it. And I'll bet he's been paying taxes longer than you've been alive.'

'Sorry, madam,' the police officer said. 'It's not my decision. It's regulations.'

The crowd began to shout. 'Cocky in, pollies out. Cocky in, pollies out!'

'Move along now quietly, please,' the officer pleaded. 'Just queue up here and you'll soon all be inside, seeing what you came to see.'

But the crowd would not move along and the children were excited. 'Cocky for Parliament!' some began calling, while others chanted, 'Cocky for Prime Minister!'

Just as one of the officers was about to call up reinforcements, a large white limousine came into sight. 'Oh no,' he said to his fellow officer. 'It's the PM himself. And TV crews following!'

The crowd milled out towards the car, which slowed down. A face everyone recognised from the TV screen in their lounge room looked out. Beside him was a woman Arthur also recognised, the Minister for Tourism and the Environment. The Prime Minister's window rolled down. 'What's all this about, Officer?'

A girl bobbed up beside the open window. 'There's a man with a cocky here. And the cocky's a living national treasure. He was born in a tree that was cut down to make way for the first Parliament House. And they won't let the man and the cocky in!'

The PM glanced at his colleague. She was looking anxiously out at the crowd. *Her* tourists – Australian, American, Japanese, German, Kiwi and Korean. What sort of message would they take home?

The PM cleared his throat. 'Well, it's regulations, you see. What if everyone wanted to bring their dog or cat or guinea pig or goldfish?'

But the girl was not going to be fobbed off with a silly answer. 'You're the Prime Minister,' she said. 'You can change the regulations.'

'Oh, it's not as easy as that,' the PM told her.

'Well, just break them once,' the girl said, swinging her long hair defiantly.

Arthur smiled at this spirited young champion. Cockawun squawked his approval and danced.

'Cocky's a good boy,' he told the PM.

The PM smiled. 'Well, just this once,' he said. 'I've got a bit of a soft spot for cockies. My grandfather used to have one. Remarkable birds, aren't they? Live to a great age, too. He'll be around in the year 2001, I'm sure. You'll have to bring him back for the celebrations.' He turned to his colleague, who was smiling also. 'Make a note of it. A great angle for tourism and the environment.' She nodded.

'What's your name and address?' he asked Arthur.

As Arthur was telling him, the TV cameras were whirring, the reporters were making notes. This was a bonus, a real human interest story, better than all the slanging matches in Parliament. This would send the ratings up. The crowd was clapping and cheering. The PM's window rolled shut. The car drove on.

Arthur and Cockawun were carried forward in the surge. They reached the door to the great building at last. The police officer was already there, talking to the security guard. Both men were smiling as Arthur checked in his swag.

Everyone was smiling as they filed in. Something to write home about.

Arthur hoped there wouldn't be any ambulances or fire engines going past, any sirens to set Cockawun wailing, especially when they were in the Chambers. They walked around with the guide in a big party, through the foyer, up stairs, along corridors, round corners, miles and miles and miles it seemed to Arthur. Past portraits and glass cases and notices and people going about their business, whatever that was. At last they were ushered into the Visitors' Gallery of the Lower House, and looked down on all the pollies sitting below.

'Be a good boy now, Cockawun,' Arthur whispered as he saw the Prime Minister standing by the table in the centre. From his perch on Arthur's shoulder Cockawun saw him, too. He raised his crest and stretched his wings. The Prime Minister looked up at the Gallery and inclined his head in recognition. But Cockawun did not utter a sound. Not until they were outside in the corridor again. Then he announced, 'Cocky's a good boy!' and all the party laughed.

'Now we'll see the real thing,' Arthur told Cockawun as they came outside into the sunshine again at last. 'The place where you were born.' He swung his swag and Cockawun took off, calling triumphantly, glad to stretch his wings and his vocal cords.

Back to the Bulga

Down the hill over the green grass Arthur walked, while Cockawun flew, gleaming against the blue sky, to the boxy white building squatting near the artificial lake.

No vestige now of the summer-gold grass and the great gum trees that had studded the sheep paddocks of 1925, though the old stone farmhouse still stood on a little peninsula across the lake. Rose gardens swept down towards the water's edge, tourists instead of sheep wandered over the grass, and the Department of Taxation now stood where the shearing sheds might have been.

Arthur walked slowly up the steps of the building he had only ever seen before in photographs. The building that had changed his life when he was a boy. While Cockawun foraged on the grass below, he stood on the steps thinking back over the years, trying to imagine what life might have been like without Cockawun. Remembering all the times they had shared. Remembering . . .

He was deep in dreaming, in another time, when suddenly he felt his ear being nibbled. Cockawun was heavy on his shoulder again. They walked to the entrance, Arthur prepared to be turned away.

But the woman behind the glass screen was smiling. 'We were hoping you would come. They rang from new Parliament House to tell us we might expect you. What a pity the cocky

can't sign the visitors' book. But you can, so please sign it for him as well. And there's no charge for such special guests,' she said as Arthur fished in his pocket.

Here the crowds were smaller, and there were no guided tours. Arthur and Cockawun could go at their own pace, pausing, looking at portraits, photos, the history and personalities of the place of Cockawun's birth and the span of his life. Arthur stood for a long time gazing at a big oil painting, a scene of summer-gold grass with sheep and a great gum tree against the backdrop of the purple mountains encircling Canberra. Another dream, another time. Until Cockawun nibbled his ear again.

On the first floor they found the National Portrait Gallery. Sportsmen and women, lawyers, writers, artists, scientists stared down at them. Arthur read the notes about them. Cocka-wun stared back at the faces with his one good eye. 'Your photo ought to be here, Cockawun,' Arthur declared. 'You belong in this lot.'

'Just what we were thinking,' a young man with a camera said behind him. Arthur turned round and the young man introduced himself.

'I'm one of the curators here. And I heard about you this morning. We'd like to take the cockatoo's photo, and if you have time, perhaps we could have a bit of a chat over a coffee.'

Cockawun posed obligingly, and afterwards they sat in an office full of filing cabinets. Cockawun demolished a biscuit while Arthur told his story, and the curator listened in fascination, his tape-recorder whirring.

Then Arthur and Cockawun went down to the souvenir shop. 'Must send young George a card,' Arthur said. He chose a picture of old Parliament House.

The woman behind the counter said, 'You've really started something. I've sold out already of postcards of sulphur-crested cockatoos and I've tried to buy some in from other sources, but everyone wants them. They're Number One today.'

Cockawun danced for her and told her what a good boy he was. She scratched behind his crest in exactly the right spot and said, 'My grandmother used to have a cocky. They're amazing birds, aren't they? Mischievous though. He was very partial to Grandpa's carnations.'

Arthur sat on the steps in the sun and pulled his pen out of his pocket. Just as he began to write to young George a flock of wild sulphur-crests flew over, calling. Cockawun took off, shrieking, 'Wait for me, wait for me.' They wheeled and came back and together they circled overhead.

Arthur felt a lump in his throat and suddenly his eyes were too blurred to see the shining white forms growing smaller against the high blue sky. It was a while before he could finish the postcard:

Wish you were here. But if you're watching TV tonight you'll see something that will surprise you. We've had a great visit. Canberra is an interesting place, like you said. We've made lots of friends and Cockawun has met his wild cousins. But it will be good to be home.

Then he sat and waited. Waited and waited, staring into the empty sky, the empty distance. He shivered on the warm step in the bright sunshine, enfolded in cold dark memories of a far-off place and a far-off time when a great tree, a tree that must never be cut down, sheltered him in a circle of stones that must never be moved. Where a white cockatoo guided him, guarded him.

At last he got slowly to his feet and walked down the steps. He looked back at the square squat building that had given him Cockawun for almost his lifetime. He looked into the distance, the empty distance. And began to walk. Towards the railway station. He had known before he left the farm that it could end like this.

The swag was light on his shoulder and his heart was heavy in his chest. A stone that could not be moved. His mouth was dry but his eyes were wet. One day he would show young George the tree and tell him that the stones must never be moved. One day. He walked on in a dream.

A shriek roused him. He looked around. Was it a dream or was it real? Cockawun was flying along Canberra Avenue towards him.

'Cockawun!' Arthur shouted, throwing his swag into the air with joy.

Cockawun swooped down onto his shoulder. They walked on together. Going home. Home to the Bulga.

About the Story

Cockawun and Cockatoo was inspired by a real cocky, pictured above, and his late owner, George Coleman, who in 1983 was one of the volunteers working to reclaim the Wingham Brush, a unique remnant of rainforest on the central NSW coast.

George took me to his home to show me some of his old photos and natural history collection. Out in the garden I met Cocky, who was busy under the macadamia tree with nuts. On my next visit a year later Cocky obviously remembered me and showed pleasure at seeing me again, even though I disturbed his session with his favourite watch.

My grandparents had a cocky and I've always been fascinated by them. I was even more intrigued with George's cocky when he told me its history.

In 1925 George's uncle had found him as a nestling in a hollow limb of a gum tree felled to clear the site for building the first Parliament House in what was to become Canberra. He had taken the baby cockies to Sydney – there were two – and given them to his nephew, George, to rear. So Cocky and George had been together since George was a boy.

When George's parents moved to Taree in 1926, Cocky and his sibling went with the family. George's father bought a little farm up in the depths of the bush on the Bulga Plateau above the Manning River.

In 1984 George took my husband and me up to the old farm, by then deserted, showed us the shimmering Ellenborough Falls and many secrets of his beloved bush, including the satin bower-bird's playground.

He pointed out the ancient Aboriginal path that crossed the mountains, and led me to an old old tree, where he was very distressed to find

Cocky with his family

that the stone circle had been disturbed. Later he took me to another place in a valley, where there was a powerful Aboriginal presence.

George also drove us down to the coast and showed us where his family used to camp.

He told anecdotes of Cocky's escapades, intelligence, cleverness – and mischief – such as are told about most cockies, and I have drawn on these and others.

Cocky was indeed shot at by a neighbour and lost the sight of one eye. He met with an untimely death, not long before George died.

As far as I know George never took Cocky back to Canberra. But it makes a good story. George, who had the love of yarns and typical dry humour of a bushman, would have enjoyed it. And the sulphur-crested cockatoos often to be seen today on the grass near old Parliament House, and flying squawking overhead, could well be some of Cocky's mob.

George Coleman as I knew him

About the Author

Christobel Mattingley has been writing since she was eight years old. Her first pieces were published in the children's pages of the *Sydney Morning Herald* and the nature magazine *Wild Life*. *Cockawun and Cockatoo* is her forty-first book. *Survival in Our Own Land*, a major work of non-fiction, also reflects her lifelong commitment to recognition of traditional ownership of Australia by Aboriginal peoples and of Aboriginal culture.

In 1990 Christobel received the Advance Australia Award for service to literature. In 1994 *No Gun for Asmir* was Highly Commended in the Australian Human Rights Awards, as was *The Race* in 1995. In 1995 Christobel was made an Honorary Doctor of the University of South Australia for her contribution to literature and social issues. In 1996 she was made a Member of the Order of Australia (AM) for service to literature, particularly children's literature, and for community service through her commitment to social and cultural issues.